ZAPATO POWER
FREDDIE RAMOS ZOOMS TO THE RESCUE

D1052109

Jacqueline Jules   art by MIGUEL BENÍTEZ

Albert Whitman & Company
Chicago, Illinois

Library of Congress Cataloging-in-Publication Data

Jules, Jacqueline.
Zapato power : Freddie Ramos zooms to the rescue / Jacqueline Jules ;
illustrated by Miguel Benítez.
p. cm.
Summary: A very unusual squirrel is spotted in and around Starwood Elementary School,
and when Freddie uses his Zapato Power to chase it,
he finds more than one opportunity to be a hero.
[1. Superheroes—Fiction. 2. Squirrels—Fiction. 3. Schools—Fiction.
4. Sneakers—Fiction. 5. Hispanic Americans—Fiction.] I. Benítez, Miguel, ill.
II. Title. III. Title: Freddie Ramos zooms to the rescue.
PZ7.J92947Zax 2011
[Fic]—dc22
2010031131

Text copyright © 2011 by Jacqueline Jules
Illustrations copyright © 2011 by Miguel Benítez
Published in 2011 by Albert Whitman & Company
ISBN 978-0-8075-9484-1

Printed in the United States of America
10 9 8 7 6 5 4 LB 20 19 18 17 16 15

The design is by Nick Tiemersma.

For more information about Albert Whitman & Company,
visit our web site at www.albertwhitman.com.

For alan, my husband and my superhero. —JJ

CONTENTS

1. A Squirrel in School..................... 1
2. A Mystery Present
   at My Door 12
3. Silver Goggles 19
4. The Storm................................. 29
5. The Man in the Yellow Vest 37
6. A Trip to the
   Principal's Office...................... 46
7. Stop the Train!.......................... 59
8. A Hero (At Last) 68

1. A Squirrel in School

"Is that a new watch?" my friend Geraldo asked as we walked into class.

"No," I said, looking down at my right arm. "Just a wristband."

"The flashing lights are cool," Geraldo said.

I covered my wrist with my left

hand. Geraldo had no idea what those clear flashing buttons could do. If I pressed one, I could zoom out of the classroom in a cloud of smoke. My wristband controlled my Zapato Power, the purple sneakers I wore to school every day, ready to be a hero.

Except there weren't too many superhero jobs at Starwood Elementary. The last person who cried "Help!" was my friend Maria, when she dropped her pencil box. Most days were filled with math, social studies, art, and other normal stuff.

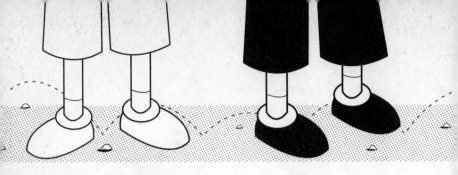

Luckily, that day was different, thanks to a gray squirrel with a long bushy tail.

We saw him, coming in from recess. He dashed right by our teacher, Mrs. Lane, as she was holding open the door.

"Look!" Maria shouted. "A squirrel!"

"**eeeeeee!**"

A squirrel running in the school sure got people excited. My class chased after it. Everyone rushed out of their classrooms to watch. The

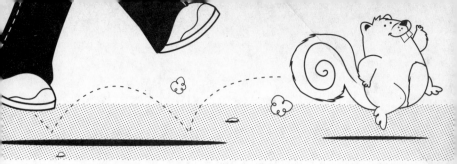

principal, Mrs. Connor, came out of her office. I smiled. This was NOT going to be another boring, quiet day at Starwood Elementary.

"STAY AWAY!" Mrs. Connor shouted. She put her hand up like a crossing guard. "SQUIRRELS CAN BE DANGEROUS!"

Dangerous? That word got my superhero radar going! I never thought I'd need to save my school from a squirrel, but any hero job was a job for me.

A long gray tail dashed around the corner. I tapped my wristband and took off.

ZOOM! ZOOM! Zapato!

My purple zapatos give me super speed. I can run faster than a squirrel. I can run faster than a train. And best of all, you only see a puff of smoke when I pass.

ZOOM! ZOOM! Zapato!

I heard more screaming and followed the noise to the music room, where kids were jumping.

"SQUIRREL!" they shouted.
"THAT WAY!"

ZOOM! ZOOM! ZAPATO!

With super speed, I could search the whole building in two blinks. The problem was finding the squirrel. Squirrels are not just fast, they're small. They can hide.

ZOOM! ZOOM! ZAPATO!

I ran through the school three times, listening for screams. No luck! I was just about to give up when

I saw a flash of gray run into the kindergarten hall. The kindergartners only go half day, so the rooms were quiet. I tiptoed through an open door. Bingo! Something gray and fluffy was sitting on the windowsill, with his paws raised, like he was begging to go outside. Poor squirrel!

ZOOM! ZOOM! ZAPATO!

I opened a window for him on the other side of the room. Now all I had to do was get him moving.

"BOO!" I stamped my foot. The squirrel ran, but towards the open

door, not the window. OOPS! I
should have thought of that.

ZOOM! ZOOM! ZaPaTO!

I slammed the door. The squirrel
spun around, saw the open window,
and escaped.

Freddie, the superhero, saved Starwood Elementary from a squirrel! I was happy until the principal charged into the room.

"Freddie Ramos," Mrs. Connor asked, "did you slam that door?"

Superheroes are supposed to work in secret. That's why so many of them have masks. I didn't have a mask, so I had to talk as fast as I could run.

"Yes, but I was helping get rid of the squirrel."

Mrs. Connor pointed to herself. "That pest is my problem, not yours, Freddie."

The principal marched me back to Mrs. Lane and told her to keep an eye on me. Secret superheroes don't get much credit.

2. A Mystery Present at My Door

With the squirrel gone, I was all out of superhero work. Mrs. Lane kept me busy with schoolwork until the bell rang. Then I ran up the stairs to Starwood Park, where my mom and I live. At my door, I saw something that made my heart beat quick—a package!

"The last time you got a present, it changed your life," a deep voice said.

I turned around to see Mr. Vaslov. He had a plunger in 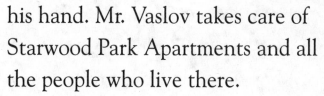 his hand. Mr. Vaslov takes care of Starwood Park Apartments and all the people who live there.

"Did you leave this for me?" I showed him my name on the thick envelope.

He chuckled and shook his bushy

gray head. "Not this time, Freddie."

Mr. Vaslov is also an inventor. He made my super zapatos. Except he wasn't sure they worked at first. He left them at my door in a box, so I could test them out.

"You can tell me the truth," I said. "I won't laugh if your new invention is a dud."

Mr. Vaslov walked away with his plunger. "Sorry, Freddie. I have to go. There's a stopped up toilet next door."

He left me alone with the padded brown envelope. I took it inside my apartment, 29G, and pulled the red strip on the bottom. Gray fluffy stuff blew into my face, and I sneezed. Not everything about getting a present is fun.

After I cleaned off my face, I put my hand in the envelope. Inside, I found a pair of super looking

GOGGLeS!

They were silver, just like the wings on the side of my purple zapatos. I ran down the hall to a mirror.

"*Fantástico!*" The silver goggles looked like a superhero mask. They were just what I wanted! And

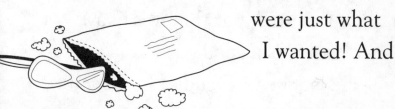

I knew just who gave them to me.

I zoomed back outside to find Mr. Vaslov. He was hurrying down the sidewalk with his plunger under his arm.

ZOOM! ZOOM! ZAPATO!

Super speed sure helps when you want to catch up with someone.

"Thanks for the silver goggles!" I said, giving Mr. Vaslov a hug. It got me a little closer to the plunger than I wanted, but that was okay. Mr. Vaslov is a good guy.

He laughed. "Freddie! I told you.

It wasn't me."

"It has to be you!" I said. "No one else knows I need them."

Mr. Vaslov rubbed his chin. "We did talk about getting you a costume."

"YES! And this is a great mask for a superhero. Thank you!"

"It wasn't me," Mr. Vaslov repeated, shaking his head. "Sorry."

I was confused. If Mr. Vaslov didn't give me the goggles, who did?

"There's the train!" Mr. Vaslov put his hand by his ear. The metro train was rumbling behind Starwood Park on its overhead track. "Are you going to race it?"

My feet tingled in my purple shoes. Racing the train always made me feel good. And it would be a chance to try out my silver goggles. I hoped they could keep the wind out of my eyes.

"See you later!" I waved at Mr. Vaslov.

ZOOM! ZOOM! Zapato!

3. Silver Goggles

The grass beside the overhead train track is the world's best place to run. I spread out my arms, pretending to be an airplane. Airplanes can beat trains, and that's how fast I am.

ZOOM! ZOOM! ZAPATO!

My legs spun faster and faster. A light cloud swirled around me. *Rápido!* The train fell behind me as the wind whooshed hard against my face. But it didn't hurt my eyes, not with the silver goggles protecting them.

ZOOM! ZOOM! ZAPATO!

I ran past the train station, down a trail that leads to a bridge over the tracks. Then I stopped and checked my watch just as the 5:35 came speeding in beneath me. That's my mom's train. I love to watch it come through. She leaves

work at the same time every day,
and walks from the station. When
she comes home she expects to
see me with open books, doing my
homework. *No hay problema.* Mom
wouldn't beat me home.

ZOOM! ZOOM! ZAPATO!

   Smoke whooshed out of my
super shoes as I ran down the trail.
Between the trees, I could see the
track getting higher as it rose to
meet the station. And I could see
the letter "W" on a red baseball cap
stuck in a tree.

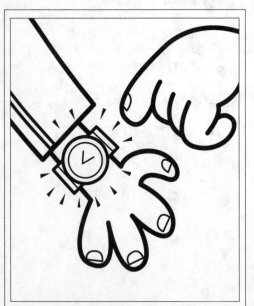

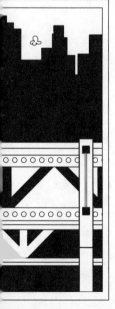

Zapato Power smoke gave me super vision, like looking through a telescope. And with my silver goggles, I didn't have to squint in the wind anymore. Next to my super sneakers, they were the best gift ever.

When I got home, my guinea pig, Claude the Second, stood up in his cage.

"WHEET!" That's Claude the Second's way of saying hello. "WHEET!"

I gave him a carrot and went to the mirror to look at my silver goggles again. Who gave them to me?

My Uncle Jorge mailed presents sometimes. I looked at the padded envelope the goggles came in. The return address was Cleveland, Ohio. Uncle Jorge lived in New York. I didn't know anybody in Ohio.

There were no clues inside the envelope, either. Just more of that gray fluffy stuff that made me sneeze.

It was a mystery I'd have to figure out after my homework.

"How was your day, Freddie?"

Mom came through the door and smiled to see me with my math book open. "Anything exciting happen?"

I told her about the squirrel. She thought it was so funny, I didn't have to add anything else, like how I got a mystery package with silver goggles. Besides, Mom was excited to show me something.

"Look what I bought for you on my lunch hour." She held up an orange bathing suit with palm trees all over it. Orange was not my favorite color, and I wasn't so sure about the palm trees, either.

"It was on sale," she said.

That didn't surprise me. Mom loved sales. But why did she get me a bathing suit?

"Where am I going to wear it?" I asked.

"Summer camp!" Mom said. "I signed you up!"

"Isn't that expensive?"

"A little," Mom admitted. "But your Uncle Jorge sent me some money to help pay for it. He wants you to learn how to swim."

"He didn't tell me that! We talked last week."

Uncle Jorge called me a couple

of times a month to ask if I was still playing basketball and wearing my hair short like a soldier. My dad was a hero in the army. And ever since we lost him, Uncle Jorge helps my mom and me out whenever he can.

"Summer will be here soon," Mom said. "Only one month."

"You're right!"

Camp didn't seem like such a bad idea. And I'd always wanted to learn how to swim. It was a good skill for a superhero to have.

4. The Storm

That night, just after I went to bed, we had a thunderstorm. It was a really loud one, the kind that sounds like horses stamping on the roof while some crazy cowboy shoots a rifle. My mom got a little scared, so I ran out of my bedroom to keep her company.

Crash! Crack!

"What was that?" Mom shouted.
I thought about putting on my

purple sneakers and silver
goggles. Superheroes are
supposed to be brave and
check out loud noises.
But it was dark outside,
and my mom looked like
she needed me.

"*No te preocupes.*" She
touched my cheek. "Don't worry.
We're together."

Another crash of thunder made us
both jump. We hugged on the couch
until all the roaring, pounding, and

booming stopped. It was nice to have a mom to take care of.

In the morning, I left the house with my purple zapatos on my feet, my wristband on my arm, and my silver goggles in my backpack. If there was a superhero job at school, I'd be ready.

Mr. Vaslov met me at the stairs leading down to Starwood Elementary.

"Look at that!" He pointed at the school.

A huge tree had fallen, hitting the edge of the gym roof, making a hole. Mrs. Connor wasn't going to be happy about this.

"The winds were really high last night," Mr. Vaslov said.

"And loud. I'm glad it's over."

"The storm is," he answered, "but not the clean up. More trees could fall."

"Really?" I asked.

Mr. Vaslov nodded. "Bad storms weaken them."

We talked about falling trees until Mr. Vaslov looked at his watch. "You're going to be late, Freddie."

"No, I'm not!" I said, taking off. "I have Zapato Power."

ZOOM! ZOOM! ZAPATO!

I walked into my classroom just as the bell rang. Everyone, including Mrs. Lane, was crowded around the window. At first we all looked at the big tree on the gym roof.

Then Geraldo shouted. "Check out that squirrel!"

"He's purple!" Jason called.

"It can't be," Maria said. "Squirrels aren't purple."

But the one standing outside our window was. His fur looked like he had fallen into a bucket of grape soda.

"He looks hungry!" Geraldo said.

His paws were raised, like he was begging. He reminded me of the gray squirrel I'd chased out of the kindergarten room.

"Why is he purple?" Maria asked. "Did someone paint him?"

"Let's hope not," Mrs. Lane

answered. "That would be cruel."

Who would hurt a squirrel?

I thought about my guinea pig, Claude the Second. He was such a small, friendly, furry guy. I'd sure be upset if someone was mean to him.

When Mrs. Lane told us to put our backpacks away and get ready

for math, I checked on my silver goggles. They were right where I left them, between my lunch and my library book. If someone was hurting little animals, I would need Zapato Power soon.

5. The Man in the Yellow Vest

I wore my goggles out to recess.
Jason noticed right away.

"Hey! Is that you, Freddie! You
look like a crime fighter!"

It was exactly what I wanted to
look like. Was it okay for kids to
see my costume? Mr. Vaslov didn't
mind if I wore my super zapatos

and my wristband to school. It was the best way to test if his inventions really worked.

But Mr. Vaslov didn't give me the goggles. That was still a mystery.

"Can I try them on?" Jason asked.

Jason cries a lot, so I let him have a turn with the goggles. It gave me a chance to see them on someone else's face. If I didn't know Jason was wearing a green shirt with blue jeans, the goggles would have been a good mask. That's what I needed. Superheroes can't do their jobs if everyone knows who they really are.

"Thanks, Freddie," Jason said,

handing back the goggles.

I put them in my pocket, deciding to be a little more careful around my friends. If they found out I had shoes with super speed, they'd be jealous. Mr. Vaslov has only been able to make one pair of special shoes and I have them.

"Look over there!" Jason shouted. "TV cameras."

We went to the gym, where Mrs. Connor was talking to TV reporters and pointing at the tree on the roof.

"Are you worried about the safety of the children?" a lady with a microphone asked.

"Of course," Mrs. Connor said. "That's all I ever worry about."

Just then, the purple squirrel popped his head out of the hole in the gym roof and scampered down the tree trunk. He stood directly in front of the TV camera.

"A purple squirrel!" the camera man squealed. "We have another news story!"

Mrs. Connor didn't want a squirrel stealing her TV time. She stamped her foot and shouted. "GO AWAY!"

That's all the purple squirrel
needed to take off. The reporters
followed him with their microphone
and camera. They couldn't keep
up—not without Zapato Power.
I pressed the first button on my
wristband and pulled out my goggles.

ZOOM! ZOOM! ZAPATO!

The problem with chasing
squirrels is that they don't run on
the ground. They scamper up trees
and fly off branches. Luckily, the
purple squirrel made a lot of noise
and his color was easy to spot.

ZOOM! ZOOM! Zapato!

I chased the purple squirrel behind the school, past Starwood Park, and through the woods. Once, I got stuck behind a big tree that had fallen in the storm. *No hay problema.* I pushed the second button on my wristband.

BOING!

I jumped right over the fallen tree. Mr. Vaslov accidentally gave me super bounce when he made me the wristband to control my sneakers. Jumping high in the air was almost like flying, except birds fly straight and I just bounce. It was faster to run.

ZOOM! ZOOM! ZAPATO!

The squirrel finally stopped just outside the gate of the metro station. He scurried up to a man in a yellow vest and raised his paws.

"You're late, little friend," the man said as he dropped some peanuts on the ground. "You almost missed your snack."

The purple squirrel grabbed a peanut and chomped away while the man leaned down for a closer look.

"Whoa!" he said. "What happened to you?"

That's exactly what I was trying to figure out.

Who would paint a squirrel purple?

6. A Trip to the Principal's Office

I left the purple squirrel with the man in the yellow vest. Recess was just about over, and I had to get back to Mrs. Lane. Teachers are like moms. They always want to know where you are.

ZOOM! ZOOM! ZaPaTO!

When I got back to the playground, I found my whole class gathered around the TV reporters, answering questions about the purple squirrel.

"When did you first see him?"

"This morning," Jason said.

"I saw him first!" Geraldo waved his arms, trying to be sure he got on TV.

"Does he live in the school?" The reporter put the microphone in front of Mrs. Lane.

"I hope not! Mrs. Connor wouldn't like that."

Did the principal hate squirrels?

She sure stamped her foot and shouted loud when the purple squirrel tried to steal her TV time. Maybe Mrs. Lane had given me a clue I should check out.

But that meant going to the principal's office! No one wants to go there. That's where teachers send you when you get caught throwing food in the cafeteria. I gulped. Superheroes sure had to be brave.

While everybody was busy talking to the TV reporters, I took the chance to get away.

ZOOM! ZOOM! ZAPATO!

In half a blink, I was outside Mrs. Connor's office. The door was open, which was lucky. Mrs. Connor was behind her desk, which was not so lucky.

"Freddie?" Mrs. Connor called when she saw me. "Did your teacher send you?"

"No." I put one purple shoe inside the room. "I just came for a visit."

Mrs. Connor was typing at her computer. "Sit down," she said.

There was a round table on the left. It had markers and coloring sheets. Was this a clue? Did my

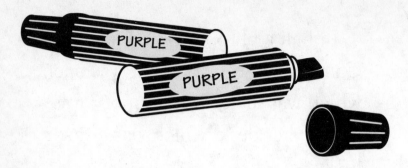

principal paint the squirrel with a purple marker?

"Do you like to color?" I asked Mrs. Connor.

She looked up from her computer. "Sometimes."

"What about squirrels?" I asked. "Do you like them?"

"No, Freddie." Mrs. Connor stood up at her desk. "I do not."

"Why?" Squirrels had cute little faces and whiskers that twitched just like my guinea pig, Claude the Second.

"Squirrels are a nuisance," she said with a frown.

Grown-ups who like little kids should like little animals, too. What was wrong with Mrs. Connor?

"So tell me why you came to visit." Mrs. Connor sat down at the table and picked up a purple marker, like she wanted to color something. I didn't want it to be me.

"No reason," I said, jumping up.

It sure felt good to know I could get away fast.

ZOOM! ZOOM! ZaPaTo!

After school, I went home, called my mom, and took care of my own little animal, Claude the Second.

CRUNCH! My guinea pig chomped on his carrot while I watched.

What could make his brown fur change color? He ate carrots every day without turning orange. Once, he chewed part of a magazine that got too close to his cage. That didn't change his color, either. If Claude the Second turned purple like the squirrel, it would have to be from something he touched, like paint or markers. Mrs. Connor—the only squirrel hater I knew—was looking guiltier by the minute.

I put on my silver goggles and looked in the mirror. Jason was right. I did look like a crime fighter. Whoever gave me my goggles wanted me to be a hero. I left 29G, ready for action.

ZOOM! ZOOM! ZAPATO!

The first place I went was Starwood Elementary. Maybe I could catch Mrs. Connor in the act.

ZOOM! ZOOM! ZAPATO!

I ran around the school, with my eyes open wide behind my goggles, looking carefully at everything. Workers had taken the tree off the gym roof and put up blue plastic. Suddenly, it started moving like someone under bed covers. A second later, the purple squirrel wiggled out and dashed down the side of the building.

ZOOM! ZOOM! ZAPATO!

I followed him through the woods, past the train station again. This time, the squirrel didn't stop to visit the man in the yellow vest. He hurried down the trail I used to see my mom's train come in from downtown. I looked at my watch. Mom's train wasn't due for another fifteen minutes.

When we got to the bridge, the purple squirrel stopped to check out a paper bag on the ground. My Zapato Power smoke was still

swirling around me and I could see his
fur clearly, even from a distance. There
were spots of gray. If Mrs. Connor did
this, she was a lousy painter.

The purple squirrel looked up.
Our eyes met. For a moment he
looked just like Claude the Second
when he's begging for a carrot.
Then he ran off. From the bridge, I
could see him scamper up a big tree
near the tracks. The tree looked

funny, like it was leaning over, sick.
I remembered what Mr. Vaslov said
about the storm and bad winds
hurting trees. Then I heard: **Crash!**
Crack!

The big tree fell, and the purple
squirrel jumped off. I didn't even
think about chasing him. I had a

much bigger problem. The tree
was lying across the tracks. A train
would be coming through soon. My
mom's train! And when it hit that
tree, it would crash!

7. Stop the Train!

What should I do? I wasn't big enough to move the tree. Somebody had to stop the train! Who?

I remembered the man in the yellow vest. If the squirrel visited him every day, he probably worked at the train station. Maybe he could help.

ZOOM! ZOOM! ZAPATO!

Most of the time when I raced, it was just a game. This time, my mom and everyone else on the train depended on me.

ZOOM! ZOOM! ZAPATO!

I stopped at the train station in a cloud of smoke. Where was the man in the yellow vest? My Zapato Power eyes spotted him just beyond the gate. You needed money to go through the gate and I didn't have any. But I did have super bounce. I pressed the second button on my wristband.

BOING!

The man in the yellow vest took a step back as I landed in a puff of smoke on his toes.

"Help!" I cried. "There's a tree on the tracks!

"Where?"

After I told him, he ran to tell another man in a blue uniform with a badge.

"A tree on the tracks!" The other man shouted. "How do you know this?"

The man in the yellow vest pointed at me. "See the kid over there? With the purple shoes and the silver goggles?"

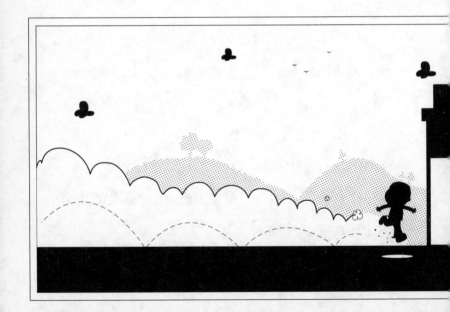

"Stop the train!" I pleaded. "It's going to crash!"

"We will," the man in the blue uniform said.

They picked up their walkie-talkies and gave all kinds of orders. I didn't stick around. The action was back at the tree down on the track halfway between this station

and downtown. Could they keep my mom's train from crashing?

Yes! I reached the bridge just in time to see the train wheels screech to a stop. A man in a uniform jumped out to look at the fallen tree over the tracks. He put his hand on his heart and opened his mouth wide. I watched with my mouth

opened, too, in a wide smile.

Sirens whistled and all kinds of officers dashed through the woods and into the train. They didn't let anybody off. I waited and wondered about my mom. Was she scared?

"It won't be too much longer, Freddie," a deep voice said.

I turned around to see Mr. Vaslov. "How did you know I was here?"

"Your mom called to check on you. She couldn't get you, so she called me."

"Is she okay?"

Mr. Vaslov nodded. "Everybody is."

"Zapato Power really helped

today," I said. I told Mr. Vaslov what happened.

"You make me proud I invented it." He put his hand on my shoulder.

Finally, the driver went to the other end of the train and drove it back downtown. My mom and all the people on the train were safe. And I was a hero.

But I hadn't told the man in the yellow vest my name. Nobody knew who saved the train, except me and Mr. Vaslov.

8. A Hero (At Last)

Mr. Vaslov drove me to the downtown station to pick up my mom. We hugged and cried and said lots of mushy stuff. Then Mom looked at me.

"Freddie? Why are you wearing silver goggles?"

My mom had just been in an almost train wreck. It didn't seem like the best time to tell her I'd gotten a gift from a stranger in Ohio, so I started slowly.

"They came in the mail," I said.

"From Uncle Jorge?" Mom asked.

"Maybe," I said. "Did he move to Ohio?"

"No." Mom laughed. "But he told me he was ordering you some super goggles on the Internet."

"So that's why they came from Ohio!" It all made sense now. "Uncle Jorge bought me goggles for summer camp."

"You're a lucky guy!" Mr. Vaslov patted my back and grinned. We both knew I would be using my silver goggles for more than just swimming lessons.

And another job was waiting for me. Could I find the purple squirrel before Mrs. Connor did?

The next morning, all I wanted to do was rescue the squirrel. But I wasn't sure how, and I was stuck in

my desk at school.

"Check the schedule on the board," Mrs. Lane said. "Math is first today, then music."

During math, I thought about the squirrel. Was he at school? I listened carefully. No one was screaming. That meant he wasn't running in the halls.

Could he be somewhere else? Where had I seen him? I saw him

once at the recess door, once in the kindergarten hall, and twice coming out of the hole in the gym roof. Maybe he liked the gym. And the gym was just around the corner from music. I slipped away, as the other kids went inside.

ZOOM! ZOOM! ZAPATO!

Outside the gym, I saw little purple dots. This had to be a clue. I went through the door.

The big room was too quiet, and

the hole in the roof wasn't pretty. No one had come in here since the tree fell. On the basketball court, I saw more purple dots. They looked like tiny feet, small enough to belong to a guinea pig—or a squirrel.

The tracks led to a heavy red curtain at the back of the gym. It was the stage. Mrs. Lane took us there sometimes for big art projects, when we needed room to spread out. Last week, my class made a teepee on the stage with a huge piece of brown paper and lots of paint. That was before the hole in the roof made the gym a dark and spooky place.

Tap! Tap! I could hear my feet echo on the floor. Tap! Tap! Wait a minute! My sneakers didn't sound like that. Somebody else was in the gym! I was being followed.

"Freddie!" Mrs. Connor turned on the light. "What are you doing here?"

Sometimes superheroes have to race to a rescue and sometimes they have to stay put. I faced Mrs. Connor.

"Looking for the purple squirrel," I said.

The principal frowned. "We already talked about this, Freddie. I told you I would take care of that pest."

I knew it! Mrs. Connor hated the squirrel, and it was up to me to save him.

Could I distract her? I pressed the top button of my wristband and dashed behind the stage curtain.

ZOOM! ZOOM! ZaPaTO!

I expected to find a purple squirrel, not a purple mess. There were tiny purple footprints everywhere—up,

down, and all around. They led to
the far corner of the stage where
I found a squirrel's nest and a
chewed plastic bottle in a puddle
of purple paint. The squirrel was
like my guinea pig who chomped
on everything he could. Claude the
Second would make a mess like this
if he didn't have to live in a cage.

"Don't get too close, Freddie!"
Mrs. Connor called. She was
behind me again, but I wasn't
worried anymore. I'd figured it out.

Mrs. Connor didn't paint the
squirrel. He painted himself.

"Do you think it's gone?" Mrs.

Connor whispered.

We heard a rustle and turned around to see the purple squirrel. He raised his purple paws like he was begging.

"**eeeeeee!**"

Mrs. Connor threw her arms in the air and ran off the stage. Her face looked like she'd just seen a werewolf.

That's when I figured out something else. Mrs. Connor didn't hate squirrels. She was afraid of them.

"Don't worry, Mrs. Connor. I know what to do."

First, I shut the gym doors.

Now the squirrel had only one way out—through the big hole in the roof. "BOO!" I stamped my foot. He climbed up to the ceiling and disappeared.

Mrs. Connor walked up to me. Her face looked better, like someone looking at a puppy, not a werewolf.

"Thanks, Freddie," she said. You're a hero."

I smiled. That was exactly what I wanted to be.

WANT MORE ZAPATO POWER?

Read the first two books about Freddie!

ZAPATO POWER: FREDDIE RAMOS TAKES OFF

One day Freddie Ramos comes home from school and finds a strange box just for him. What's inside? **ZAPATO POWER**—shoes that change Freddie's life by giving him super speed!

ZAPATO POWER: FREDDIE RAMOS SPRINGS INTO ACTION

Freddie Ramos is back, now with even more **ZAPATO POWER!** Can he figure out how to use his zapatos in time to save a friend?

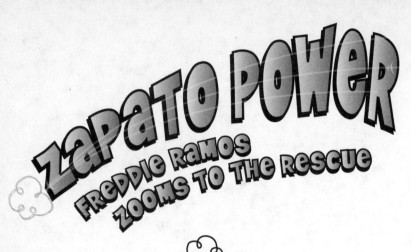

ZAPATO POWER
FREDDIE RAMOS ZOOMS TO THE RESCUE

When a freak spring blizzard buries Starwood
Park, Freddie works with Mr. Vaslov to clear the
sidewalks using a new invention—
Zapato Power snowshoes!

HC 9780807594872
$14.99/$16.99 Canada
PB 9780807594964
$4.99/$5.99 Canada